This book belongs to:

_____

Based on the TV series *Blue's Clues* ® created by Traci Paige Johnson,
Todd Kessler, and Angela C. Santomero as seen on Nick Jr. ®
On *Blue's Clues*, Steve is played by Steven Burns.
On *Blue's Clues*, Joe is played by Donovan Patton. Photos by Joan Marcus.

SIMON SPOTLIGHT
An imprint of Simon & Schuster Children's Publishing Division
1230 Avenue of the Americas, New York, New York 10020
Manufactured in the United States of America
First Edition 10 9 8 7 6 5 4 3 2 1
ISBN-13: 978-1-4169-1332-0
ISBN-10: 1-4169-1332-7
These titles were previously published individually by Simon Spotlight.

Growing Up with Blue

A 10th Anniversary Story Collection

SIMON SPOTLIGHT/NICK JR.

New York   London   Toronto   Sydney

A special letter from the creators of *Blue's Clues*

To Parents,

Wow! We can't believe that *Blue's Clues* is turning ten! Over the past ten years we packed all of our books and television shows with everything we ever wanted preschoolers to know. Through all of the games and clue finding on *Blue's Clues*, our goal was to teach preschoolers that they can do anything that they want to do. We wanted to create stories that would embrace a preschooler's view on life. It's a big deal when your friend comes over to play. A preschooler has a lot of questions when they go to the doctor for a checkup. What does Blue do when she has a sniffly day? How does Magenta feel when she has to get glasses? In order to maintain the integrity and curriculum of *Blue's Clues*, we thoroughly research everything we write about. Our research helps us stay true to the *Blue's Clues* mission: to empower, challenge, and build the self-esteem of preschoolers . . . all while making them laugh!

Through Blue, we want kids to have a friend who they can learn from and feel good about modeling. If Blue can do it, so can you! Thank you for inviting Blue into your homes for ten years and for loving the little blue puppy as much as we do.

All the best,
Angela and Traci

Table of Contents

Off to School with Periwinkle and Blue

adapted by Alison Inches
based on the teleplay by Alice Wilder
illustrated by Jennifer Oxley

It was Periwinkle's first day of school.

"I'm really excited!" he said to Blue and Joe. "But I'm a little nervous, too."

He was glad that they were coming with him.

"Let's go!" Periwinkle said as he hopped out the door.

"*To school we go, to school we go—it's off to school we go!*" they sang as they walked.

But when Periwinkle saw his school, he stopped singing.

"Will school be okay?" he asked.

"I have a great time at school," said Blue.

But Periwinkle still wasn't sure about school. He wondered what the classroom would be like. Would his teacher be nice? Would he make new friends?

"What if I don't like school?" asked Periwinkle.

"Well," said Joe thoughtfully, "do you like to paint pictures? Or read stories? Or build things with blocks?"

"Yes," said Periwinkle. "I like to do all those things!"

"Then I bet you're going to *love* school!" said Joe.

In the classroom Periwinkle's teacher introduced herself. "Welcome to school, Periwinkle. I'm Miss Marigold," she said. Then she asked Blue to show Periwinkle the cubbies.

"Which one is mine?" asked Periwinkle.

"The one with your picture on it," said Blue.

Periwinkle looked at all the cubbies. "Hey, that's me!" he exclaimed when he saw his picture.

Blue and Periwinkle put their lunch boxes in their cubbies.

Miss Marigold clapped her hands. "Okay, it's Circle Time!" she said.
"Let's all sit in a circle on the rug." Periwinkle sat next to Blue.

"We have someone new today," said Miss Marigold.

"This is Periwinkle."

"Hi, Periwinkle!" said the whole class, smiling at him.

Periwinkle blinked and smiled back.

"It's time to play the name game," said Miss Marigold. "Pick a color from the pile. Then say your name and your favorite color."

Blue went first. "I'm Blue, and blue is my favorite color!" she said.

Next it was Periwinkle's turn. "I'm Periwinkle! And my favorite color is red!" he said.

"Red is my favorite color too!" said Purple Kangaroo.

Wow, thought Periwinkle. Someone likes the same thing I like!

After Circle Time, Periwinkle learned that everyone had a special job.
Periwinkle looked at the job board and saw that his job was to feed Giggles,
the rabbit.

"I've never fed a rabbit before," said Periwinkle. "I'm not sure what to do."

"There's a sign above the cage," Miss Marigold said.

Periwinkle looked at the sign. "It says Giggles gets three cups of food."

"That's right," said Miss Marigold, and they measured the pellets together.

"One, two, three!" exclaimed Periwinkle as he put the pellets in Giggles's cage.

At recess everyone went outside. The playground had lots of great stuff—
even a water table. Periwinkle liked to race the boats and splash them into
the water.

"Stop it, Periwinkle!" said Orange Kitten. "You're getting us all wet!"

Periwinkle looked at his wet classmates.

"Sorry," said Periwinkle. "I'll try to be more careful."

After that they all had a better time at the water table.

When they came inside it was time to paint. But Periwinkle wanted to play with blocks.

"Right now it's Painting Time," said Miss Marigold.

"But I *really* want to play with blocks," said Periwinkle.

"You can play with blocks tomorrow," said Miss Marigold. She pointed to the schedule. "Can you tell me what it's time for now?" she asked.

"It's time to paint!" Periwinkle said excitedly. He put on a smock and swished paint across his paper. Then Joe walked in to check on Periwinkle.

"That's a nice painting," said Joe.

"Thanks," said Periwinkle. "It's Painting Time!"

At lunch Periwinkle sat at the lunch table with his classmates. They all had different things in their lunch boxes.

"I have a brownie!" said Green Puppy.

"I have a cookie!" said Periwinkle.

"Want to trade desserts?" asked Green Puppy.

"Sure!" said Periwinkle.

Then it was time to go home.

"But I don't want to go home!" said Periwinkle.

"You don't?" said Joe. "That must mean you liked school."

"I did! I liked it ALL! School is cool!" said Periwinkle.

"And I can't wait to come back tomorrow!"

Magenta's Visit

by Alice Wilder and Michael T. Smith
illustrated by Traci Paige Johnson and Karen Craig

Hi! It's me, Steve! We're so glad you're here today. Guess who else is here? It's someone special!

Magenta! Magenta is here! Hey, Magenta, what is your favorite
thing to do? Oh, we'll play Blue's favorite game Blue's Clues to
figure out what Magenta's favorite thing to do is.
Maybe Shovel and Pail want to play too. Let's go see.

43

You found everyone! Good job. Magenta, is hide-and-seek your favorite thing to do?

No, no, no.

That's not your favorite? Wait a second . . .
did you find a clue? It's macaroni! Hmm. Maybe
Magenta's favorite thing to do is in the kitchen.
Let's look in there!

Mr. Salt and Mrs. Pepper are making animals out of food.

We made a turtle! Now let's make a pig and an ostrich. Which foods should we use?

Wow! Can you figure out how they made these animals?
Hey, Magenta, is this your favorite thing to do?

No, no, no.

What can it be? Oh, here's our second clue! It's a frame. Maybe Magenta's favorite thing to do is in the living room. Come on!

What can Magenta's favorite thing to do be? Maybe the Felt Friends have an idea.

We're playing dress-u... Can you help us figure out which costumes go together?

Great costumes! Magenta, is playing dress-up your favorite
thing to do?

No, no, no.

Hey, look at all these pictures. Let's
see where they're coming from.

53

Tickety, were you taking pictures?

55

Oh, that's what those pictures are. It looks like you got a little too close, Tickety. Magenta, is taking pictures your favorite thing to do?

No . . . oh, wait! Here's our third clue. It's glue. We have all three clues! Now where do we go?

The Thinking Chair! Now that we're in our thinking chair, let's think. The clues are macaroni, a picture frame, and glue.

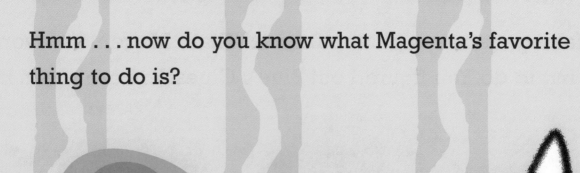

Hmm . . . now do you know what Magenta's favorite thing to do is?

Making macaroni picture frames! That's Magenta's favorite thing to do. You figured out Blue's Clues. You are so smart!

by Angela C. Santomero
Illustrated by Traci Paige Johnson and Soo Kyung Kim

It's Blue's birthday! Thank you so much for coming early to the party. We could sure use your help getting everything ready. Will you help us?

Blue, what do you really, really want for your birthday?

Oh! Blue's Clues! We are going to play Blue's Clues! Do you know how to play? Great! Blue's pawprints will be on three clues, and the clues will tell us what she really wants for her birthday!

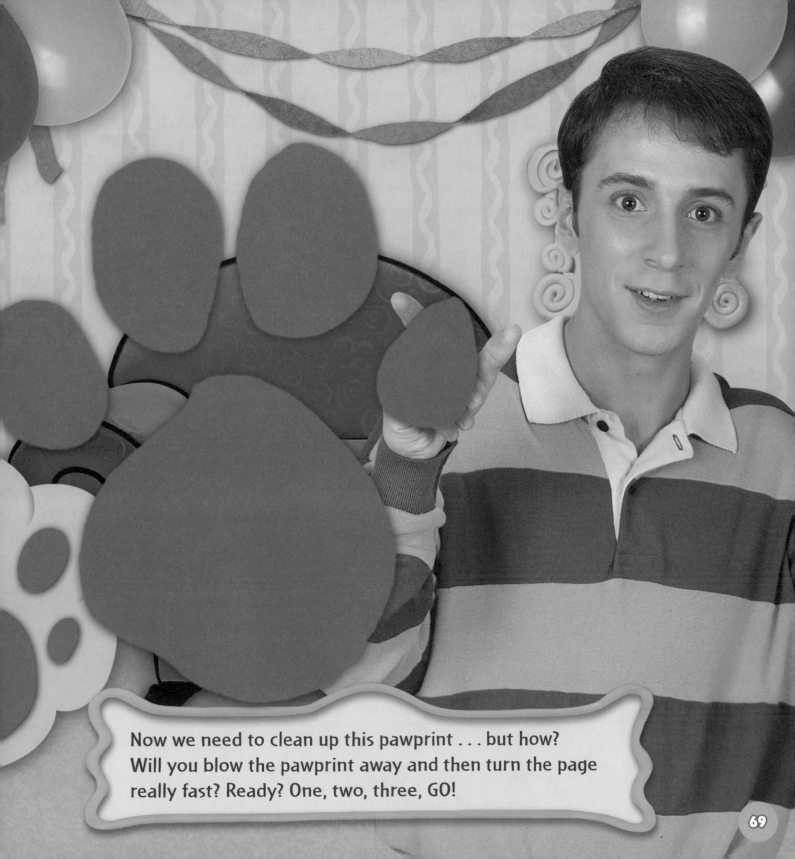

Now we need to clean up this pawprint . . . but how?
Will you blow the pawprint away and then turn the page
really fast? Ready? One, two, three, GO!

69

The pawprint is gone! Good job! Now let's find Blue's clues—keep an eye out for them!

Our first clue! And it's the color . . . do you know what color this is?
Green! We need to write down this clue in our handy-dandy notebook!

Will you help us bake our special cake for Blue's birthday? This is the recipe.

72

How many blueberries do we need? How many eggs?

How much milk do we need?

Do you want to help? Look around the kitchen and try to find all of the things we need for Blue's special cake.

73

Hey, look at that! You found all of the ingredients!
Mr. Salt and Mrs. Pepper are mixing them up!
Mixa, mixa, mixa. Poura, poura, poura. Baka, baka, baka—
Blue's birthday cake!

We'll check on Blue's birthday cake later. Did you find our second clue? Me too! I put it in my handy-dandy notebook already! Let's set the party table now, okay? We'll need ten of everything, since there will be ten of us at the party. Will you help me count ten spoons and bring them outside? You will? Thanks!

Thank you for bringing out all ten spoons! You are a really good counter! I set the party table for all of our guests. Would you check the table and see if I forgot anything? Oh! I think one of our balloons is missing. And a star lantern, too! Do you know which ones?

You were really good at finding those missing things. We put some more birthday decorations around too. Do you see what we've added? Oh! We found our third clue! A shell! You know what that means: We are ready for our . . . thinking chair! Let's go!

Do you remember what our three clues were? The color green, a fish tank, and a shell. So, what could Blue want for her birthday that is the color green, can be in a fish tank, and lives in a shell?

Blue wants a **turtle** for her birthday! That's the answer to Blue's Clues, because . . . most turtles are the color green . . . and can be in a fish tank . . . and live in a shell! We just figured out Blue's Clues!

Dingdong. That's the doorbell! The rest of our party guests must be here! Let's go have Blue's birthday party!

I'm so excited! I just love birthdays! Do you know all of Blue's friends who came to the party? Can you guess which friend gave Blue which present? Do you see the special birthday cake we helped Mr. Salt and Mrs. Pepper make?

Thank you so much for coming and helping
with the party.

You made Blue's day special!

Blue's Clues

Blue's Sniffly Day

89

by Brigid Egan
illustrated by Victoria Miller

Hi! Have you seen Blue? She's been under the weather for a few days, and we want to find out how she's feeling.

We thought you might want to play, Blue. But it doesn't look like your sniffles have gone away yet.

What can we do to make Blue feel better?

Look, Blue! Dr. Shovel and Nurse Pail are making a house call.

Can you spot anything in the room that Shovel and Pail might need for their pretend doctor's visit?

Hmm . . . it looks like Dr. Shovel and Nurse Pail's pretend checkup isn't going to help cure Blue's real cold.

Maybe Mailbox has something to make Blue feel better.

What a nice card! It really helped to cheer Blue up.

Blue is going to take a nap now. But after all that sneezing, she
wants to wash her hands first.

Good idea, Blue!
I'll help you.

Can you tell which towels belong to Blue?

You know, when I don't feel well, I like to hold Horace, my anteater. Horace always makes me feel better.

Let's see if we can find a stuffed animal for Blue to hold. Do you see any?

Maybe reading a story will help Blue feel better. Is that a good idea, Blue? Blue?

Blue's asleep! Well, maybe sleeping will make her feel better.

We can all try to be very, very quiet so Blue can sleep.
How quiet can you be?

This quiet?

Even quieter.

You're so good at being quiet! Why don't we tiptoe down to the kitchen and see what Mr. Salt, Mrs. Pepper, and Paprika are up to? Come on.

Will you help us find the rest of the ingredients from Mr. Salt's recipe? You will? Great!

NOODLES

Orange Juice

We want to give Blue the biggest bowl of soup. Can you find the biggest bowl?

Soup's ready!

Let's pour some orange juice for Blue. Can you find an orange cup for her juice? What else should we put on her tray?

I think sleeping made Blue feel a little better. Now she's ready to enjoy the soup we made. Thanks for helping Blue to feel better!

by Deborah Reber
illustrated by Troy Dugas

One day Magenta went to visit Steve and Blue.

"Oh, hi, Magenta! Aren't you going to the eye doctor today?" Steve asked.

Magenta nodded. "Why do I have to get glasses?" she sighed as she went inside. "None of my friends wear glasses."

"Do you want to help us with this puzzle, Magenta?" Steve asked.

Magenta nodded happily.

But Magenta couldn't see the puzzle pieces clearly. She squinted and squinted, but it was no use. She couldn't see well enough to help finish the puzzle.

"What's the matter, Magenta?" asked Steve. "Don't you feel like playing?"

Magenta shrugged. "I wish everything wasn't so blurry," she told her friends.

While Steve and Blue worked on the puzzle Magenta wondered what her eye exam would be like. I hope the doctor is nice, she thought.

Soon it was time to leave. Magenta was feeling a little nervous, but Steve knew how to make her feel better. "Would it help if Blue and I came along?" he asked. Magenta nodded.

"Don't worry," Steve told her. "When you get your glasses you'll be able to see perfectly!"

Maybe getting glasses won't be so bad, Magenta decided. She smiled at Steve and Blue and said, "Let's go!"

As they walked to the eye doctor's office Blue spotted a bird high in a tree. Magenta squinted and squinted, but she couldn't see the bird among the leaves. I wish I could see the bird, thought Magenta.

Then Steve and Blue saw a pretty butterfly. But no matter how hard Magenta tried, she couldn't see it. "When I get my glasses, maybe I'll be able to see the butterfly too," Magenta said to herself.

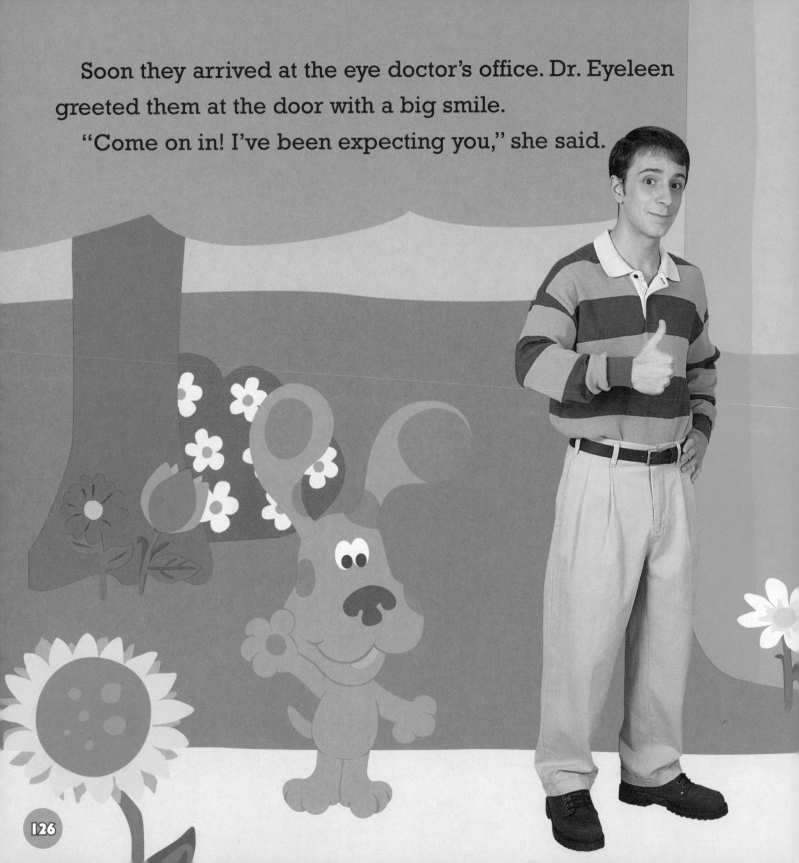

Soon they arrived at the eye doctor's office. Dr. Eyeleen greeted them at the door with a big smile.

"Come on in! I've been expecting you," she said.

As Magenta, Blue, and Steve walked inside, Dr. Eyeleen showed Magenta all of her knobs and levers. "These will help me figure out what kind of glasses you need so you can see better," she explained.

Magenta sat in the doctor's big chair and looked at a blurry chart on the wall in front of her. Then Dr. Eyeleen moved a screen in front of Magenta's eyes and started to move her knobs and levers. Suddenly Magenta could see the letters on the chart perfectly!

"Will I be able to see like this with my new glasses?" Magenta asked.

"Of course," said Dr. Eyeleen.

Magenta could hardly believe it. Now I'll be able to see the birds and the butterflies! she thought.

Soon the eye exam was over. "You did great, Magenta! Why don't you pick out some frames for your new glasses?" suggested Dr. Eyeleen.

Magenta and Blue walked over to the display and looked at all the different frames.

Magenta wanted a pair that was purple and round. She looked and looked. Finally she spotted the perfect pair.

"Here they are!" said Magenta excitedly.

Dr. Eyeleen took the purple frames out of the display and went to get Magenta's new glasses ready.

A few minutes later Dr. Eyeleen came back with the glasses. Magenta closed her eyes and put them on.

"They feel kind of funny . . . and heavy!" she said.

"Don't worry, you'll get used to the way they feel," said Dr. Eyeleen. "But how does everything *look?*"

Magenta opened her eyes. Everything looked so clear! She went over to the window and looked outside. She couldn't believe how well she could see!

"Take a look, Magenta," Blue said, holding up a mirror. A big smile spread across Magenta's face. She looked so different! But she liked what she saw.

"You look great!" said Steve. "Let's go show everyone your new glasses!"

Steve, Blue, and Magenta thanked Dr. Eyeleen and started on their way home. Magenta could see everything! "Look at that cloud!" she said.

A little farther down the path they came upon a flower patch.
"I can see bumblebees in the flowers!" Magenta said with a grin.

And as they continued on their walk home, Magenta pointed out everything she saw along the way. All with the help of her new glasses!

by Sarah Albee
illustrated by Ian Chernichaw
based on the teleplay by Jessica Lissy

"Are you ready for your doctor's appointment, Blue?" asked Joe.

Today was the day for Blue's checkup with Dr. Maya.

"I guess so," said Blue. But she didn't sound too sure.

Blue was feeling a tiny bit nervous about her checkup.
"I wonder what will happen during my visit," she said quietly.
"What will Dr. Maya do?"

"Let's pack some things to play with in the waiting room," Joe suggested.

"I'll bring Polka Dots and my doctor's bag," Blue said. "And Boris can come along too."

When they got to Dr. Maya's office, Joe said, "Well, here's the waiting room. So, let's wait!"

"We can play doctor while we're waiting," said Blue, taking out her doctor bag.

"Okay," said Joe, grinning. "Doctor! Doctor! My duck has an earache!"

Blue looked into Boris's ear with a special instrument. "I'll
have him feeling better in a jiffy," she said as she bandaged
Boris's ear.

"Thanks, Dr. Blue," said Joe.

Then it was Joe's turn to be the patient. "Doctor!" he cried. "I feel sick."

"Hmmm," said Dr. Blue. "I think you have a temperature. Take a nap, and call me tomorrow."

Just then they heard Nurse Kenny calling Blue's name. It was her turn to go into the examining room.

First, Nurse Kenny checked to see how tall Blue had grown. Then he weighed her. "You are growing very nicely, Blue," said Nurse Kenny. "You are two feet tall. And you weigh twenty pounds."

Next Nurse Kenny checked Blue's blood pressure. He wrapped a cuff around Blue's arm and pumped air into it. Then he listened carefully to Blue's heartbeat.

"Does that hurt, Blue?" asked Joe.

Blue shook her head and giggled. "It feels like the cuff is hugging my arm."

Dr. Maya came in. "Hello, Blue! Hello, Joe!" she said. She washed and dried her hands at the sink, and then she put on her stethoscope. Dr. Maya asked Blue to take deep breaths as she listened carefully to Blue's chest and back. "Your heart and lungs sound terrific! Would you like to listen too, Joe?" asked Dr. Maya.

Joe put on the stethoscope. "Wow! I hear your heart!" he said excitedly. "It sounds like this, Blue: '*Lub-dub, lub-dub!*'"

"This is an otoscope," Dr. Maya explained. "Would you like to turn on the light?"

Blue pressed the switch, and a little light went on.

"It's dark inside your body. This light helps me see what's going on in there," said Dr. Maya as she peeked into Blue's ears, eyes, and mouth.

Next Dr. Maya asked Blue to lie back on the table. She pressed Blue's tummy all over, very gently. Then she helped Blue sit up again.

"You are such a good patient!" Dr. Maya exclaimed. "We are almost done with your checkup. The last thing we need to do is give you a shot.

"A shot?" Blue asked nervously.

"Yes, Blue. The medicine inside the shot will help to keep you from getting sick," explained Dr. Maya. "You will only feel a tiny pinch. We'll count together like this: one, two, three, pinch—then it's over."

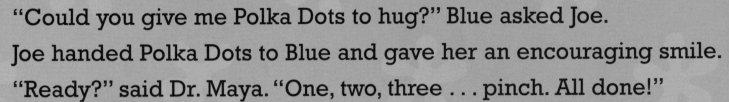

"Could you give me Polka Dots to hug?" Blue asked Joe.

Joe handed Polka Dots to Blue and gave her an encouraging smile.

"Ready?" said Dr. Maya. "One, two, three . . . pinch. All done!"

"Hey, that wasn't so bad!" said Blue.

Joe started to pack up their backpack while Dr. Maya reviewed another folder.

"Wait, don't go quite yet," Dr. Maya said as she read it over. "Hmmm. Joe, it seems that *you* are due for a booster shot today."

"Me? A shot?!" asked Joe, surprised.

Nurse Kenny led him over to the examining table and cleaned his arm with a cotton ball.

"Here's Boris to hug," said Blue.

"Well," said Joe, "if Blue can be brave, then so can I." He clutched Boris tightly.

"Ready?" asked Dr. Maya. "One, two, three . . . pinch. All done!"

"You're right, Blue," said Joe. "That really wasn't so bad!"

"Good job!" said Dr. Maya. "Be sure to get a sticker at the front desk on your way out."

"You were very brave, Blue," said Joe.

"Thanks," said Blue. "So were you!"

"Thanks. Doctor Maya's a pretty cool doctor." Joe grinned.

"Come on. Let's go show everybody our stickers!"

A Visit from the Tooth Fairy

by Sarah Albee
illustrated by Karen Craig

One morning, while Blue was brushing her teeth, she suddenly noticed a funny feeling in her mouth. One of her teeth was moving a little! She wiggled it back and forth, slowly at first, and then a bit faster.

"I have a loose tooth!" she said excitedly. Then she dashed off to find Joe.

"Wow, you have a loose tooth?" asked Joe in amazement. "Why is it loose?"

"Blue's tooth is ready to come out," explained Mrs. Pepper.

"What will you do with your tooth after it comes out?" Joe wondered.

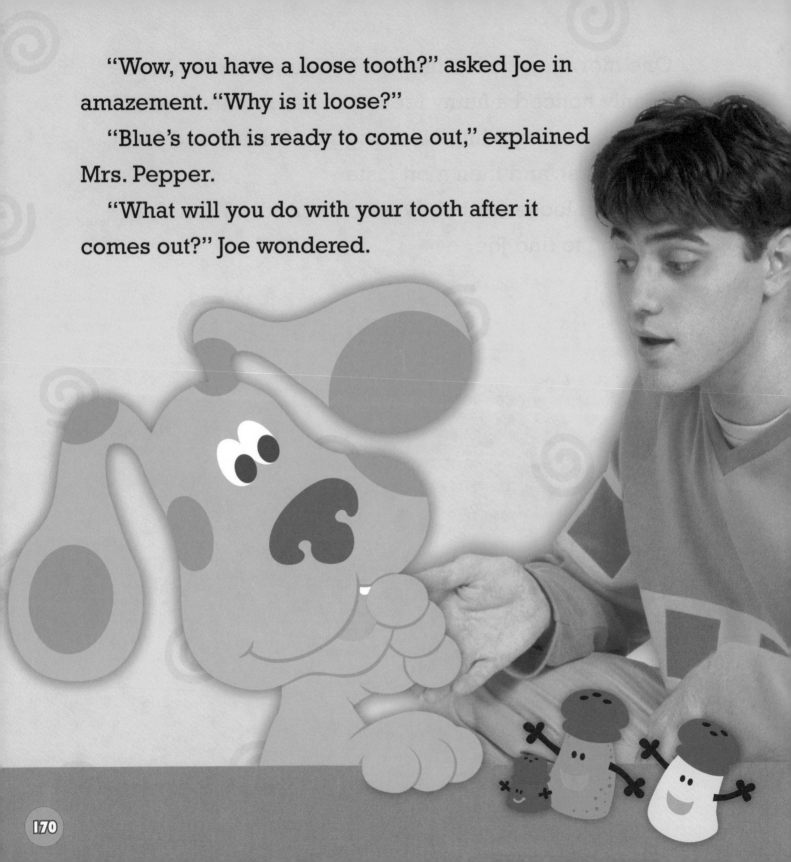

"I'll put it under my pillow," said Blue, "so the Tooth Fairy can come!"

At school that day Blue proudly showed her loose tooth to Miss Marigold. Then she showed her friends.

"Does it hurt?" asked Periwinkle.

"Not a bit," Blue replied.

"Will it hurt when it comes out?" asked Magenta.

Blue looked a little worried. "I don't think so," she said.

"I guess we'll have to wait and see."

"Have you ever seen the Tooth Fairy?" asked Green Puppy.

"No," Blue replied. "I wonder what she looks like."

"Why don't we draw some pictures of what we think the Tooth Fairy looks like?" Miss Marigold suggested. So that's what the class did.

175

Every day Blue's tooth got a little looser.

She wiggled it while she read.

She wiggled it while she played.

She even wiggled it
while she took a bath.

After a few more days Blue's tooth became so loose she could wiggle it with her tongue.

And then during Music Time, it happened! Blue was wiggle-wiggle-wiggling her tooth when suddenly . . . it fell out! And it didn't hurt a bit!

Miss Marigold put Blue's tooth in a special box so Blue could keep it safe.

Blue proudly showed her friends the tooth. She showed them the space where the tooth used to be. It was fun to feel the empty place with her tongue.

"Soon a grown-up tooth will begin to grow in the space where you lost your baby tooth," said Miss Marigold.

"This is so exciting!" said Joe when he saw Blue's tooth. "Do you think the Tooth Fairy will really come tonight?"

"I hope so," said Blue. "But Miss Marigold says no one knows what she looks like, because she only comes if you're asleep."

Before she went to bed that night Blue put her tooth under her pillow.

That night Blue had a dream. She dreamed the Tooth Fairy came to visit her.

"Hello, Blue," said the Tooth Fairy. "What a big girl you are to have lost a tooth!"

Blue smiled to show the Tooth Fairy the space where her tooth had been.

The Tooth Fairy reached under Blue's pillow and pulled out the tooth. "Well!" she said delightedly. "This is a very lovely tooth!"

"Thanks!" said Blue.

"I will take good care of it," said the Tooth Fairy as she carefully placed the tooth in her special pouch. Then she waved her wand and disappeared in a cloud of sparkly dust.

When Blue woke up the next morning the first thing she did was feel under her pillow.

"The Tooth Fairy came! The Tooth Fairy came!" she shouted. "She took my tooth and left me a surprise!"

Blue dashed away to tell Joe.